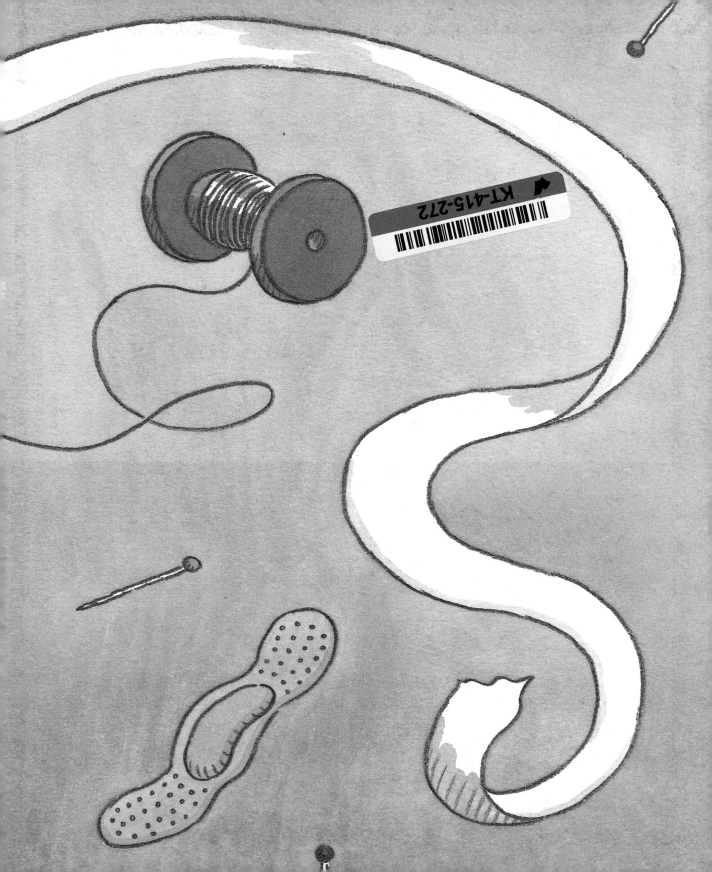

First published 1991
by Walker Books Ltd, 87 Vauxhall Walk
London SE11 5HJ

© 1991 Dom Mansell

First printed 1991
Printed and bound in Italy by
L.E.G.O., Vicenza

British Library Cataloguing in Publication Data
Mansell, Dom
My old teddy.
I. Title
823.914 [J]

ISBN 0-7445-2122-X

My Old Teddy

Dom Mansell

WALKER BOOKS
LONDON

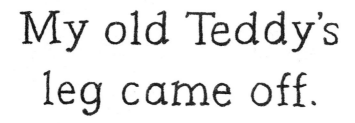

My old Teddy's
leg came off.

Poor old Teddy!

I took him to the Teddy doctor.

She made Teddy better.

My old Teddy's arm came off.

Poor old Teddy!

I took him to the Teddy doctor.

She made Teddy better.

My old Teddy's ear came off.

Poor old Teddy!

I took him to the Teddy doctor.

She made Teddy better.

Then poor old Teddy's head came off.

The Teddy doctor
said Teddy's had
enough now...

Teddy has to rest.

The Teddy doctor gave me...

my new Teddy.

I love new Teddy
very much,

but I love
poor old Teddy best.
Dear old,
poor
old
Teddy.